Reprobates

Lula Lucent

Ghost Festival Press

REPROBATES

Part of the Reprobates™ series, Novella the First

Published by Ghost Festival Press

Cover art by Les Solot

ISBN: 978-0-9906078-5-4

First edition: August 15, 2022
Duggery Day

Printed on Earth

That which harvests and is harvested.

They emerged from Hell's Reprieve, striding through the Gate to survey what only eyes bereft of redemption might see. We did not know this fact until the very end. Only once their terrible ascension was complete and their myriad sins had settled deep roots into the thrice-raped dirt was there time to reflect on what had been and all that had been lost. By then, the Earth lay ruined – and Daeli was dead.

But where was the Beast, the Guardian of the Gate, who was meant to contain them? The abomination of whom a religion was erected in ancient days until it crumbled under the weight of its own repugnance? Where was this creature whose cruelties, they say, made damnation feel a blessing?

In the Month of Ash – far too late – the seers had amassed sufficient power to glimpse Hell's antechamber. Those that survived the attempt spoke in bloody poetry before succumbing to a raving, wasting death – their souls untethered, snapping in a gale none but they could feel.

Of broken jaw all teeth unmoored; the splayed chest blooms a rotten rose; tendons spiderwebbing sun-scorched mud; our water-parched screams sing a glory of gore, O Glory: sing of our nothingness.

And then they wailed: "Who is like unto the Beast? Who can stand against it?"

The Harbingers of the Apocalypse.

Their names unknown; their mantles we know:

DEATH

PESTILENCE

FAMINE

WAR

Although I am
unequal to the task
I will now mark
the hours of the fall.

May we learn from our failures.

Reprobates

The First Seal

Atop the pinnacle of Mount Ordeal, they enter our world while it slumbers in ignorance. This is the first impossibility of their existence: they exit the Gate of Hell, that which can only accept the damned and never expel. The natural order has already been undone.

God of All Creation, who molded the clay of reality, why did you forsake us at this moment?

Woe that day. Woe unto humanity.

Woe to the beauty of that morn, its cobalt skies so clear and crisp with dawn's vulnerable arms spread wide in welcome. How could it have known? How could we?

I lament the day in God's absence.

For that pristine sunrise allowed the Harbingers to gaze upon the full expanse of the lands below, to divide in their minds the regions they would pass on through one by one. Not to conquer, but to decimate.

The spine of Ordeal, a craggy staircase lain before their cloven hooves, plunged steadily into Willow Way whose countless trees would soon weep. Glassmere, the untarnished lake whose glacial waters quenched the thirst of all races, would soon putrefy. The plains of Inirnith, where humans made their kingdom and traded wheat to placate their enemies, would burn unending. The metal desert of Kharhoom, where no one dwelled, would melt. And high above them all floated clouds that too would not be spared.

And the Harbingers, knowing this, laugh.

Horrible hollow chortles, echoing from exposed ribcages and resonating within their misshapen, horned skulls. One of them recovers and speaks in the warbling, scratchy whisper that they each masquerade as a voice.

"What a reckoning there shall be, my brother-sisters."

It is less a commentary than it is an edict, an oath, a desperate need. For though they plan to subvert everything they see into vitreous wasteland, this is only a means to their ultimate, blasphemous aim.

They will rip God from the Throne of Highest Heaven, take Its authority for themselves, and murder It without hesitation or remorse. For as they were damned from the moment they were born for the sin of existence, they will bring judgement upon It that damned them.

"O, how I long for Its end."

"The ending! The ending!"

"The Grand Catharsis, dear my sister-brothers."

They point the gaping sockets of the skulls – empty pits that should house eyes – at the Gate of Hell, raise their fists of bone, and reduce the Gate to jagged splinters. This savagery and childish rage against the inanimate belies one simple truth: they can scarcely control their emotions, and the pent-up frustration of ages can no more be contained than the brilliance of the sun. Of these splinters they fashion scythes, imbued with a portion of their respective evils.

Death holds aloft Bitterwail, pulsing with Doom.

Pestilence wields Liferot, festering with Plague.

Famine clutches Ashenhew, wracked with Wither.

War hefts Marrowcleave, exsanguinating with Blood.

This hour was approaching and is now come round at last. Lamentation unto Ordeal! Lament, you beings and creatures of the light, for the spine of your world that is so sundered! Never has hatred so struck the Earth as now strike the Harbingers' scythes upon Ordeal.

Four evil magicks twisting into a single penetration of rape. This is the first! There will be two more! O humanity, do you not feel the mountains trembling at the violation? This is not an earthquake. This is more. This is unspeakable. Daeli, who will be called Lightbringer, feels it: even now, she is staring at the morning light sparkling through the slats of her window in a hut on the plains outside the human kingdom of restless winds; and now she trembles too at an emotion she will waken to yet in an epiphany that will cost her everything precious.

The first seal is broken.

Lament as I do.
There will be more.
This end is one that lingers.

And so ossification begins:

> *A ponderous pace the mute stone*
> *disintegrates in   uneven patches*
> *like organs sloughing from   within*
> *rather than   skin from without.*
>> *Cleft holes, spheres of   nothingness*
>> *expand and do   not contract;*
>> *the rock hollowed leaving*
>> *what looks like*
>>> *connective tissue in a*
>>> *mummified   corpse*
>>> *forced   to stand*
>>> *never to be   interred.*
>>>> *These myriad holes*
>>>> *a hole in   my heart*
>>>> *where not even blood*
>>>> *dares   scream.*

So finished, the Harbingers trek down the mountainside with scarce a thought for what is happening beneath their passing. The holes continue to spread from the very peak of Ordeal down to its deepest roots. And what of the demons safely ensconced in bedrock tunnels and caverns therein who, millennia ago, were confined there after unending battles with the Fallen angelic choir? What of this subterranean scourge that a century ago sought peace with mortal kin once their hot rages had cooled from the silence and the darkness underground? They flee to the wakening world. The sun, unknown for generations, restokes their primordial fury.

Strife begins anew.

The Second Seal

And so the Harbingers descend into Willow Way. The forest, as a whole, senses the intrusion. Each root of every tree shrinks away as autonomic as the crown shyness overhead. Dappled light sprinkles down through the branches like holy rain, recalcitrant and unrelenting, with whispers in the wind of a rising protector.

Near at hand there is another whisper; for as these woods know what is abhorrent, they likewise know what is their own. The frightened roots whisper to the thickets; the thickets whisper to the ferns; the ferns whisper to the moss and lichen and toadstools, and this collective rhizome whispers loudly to any living thing that does not yet hear and listen to the echo of coming calamity. Soon, all within Willow Way know and the faefolk reach for weapons of war.

And were the Harbingers lesser, this may have been enough. But this aggression, this pulse within the forest, this movement as perilous as the quaking of Ordeal, is a heartbeat that War perceives and perceives well.

"We are seen," War croaks. "We will be met." And plunging Marrowcleave into the nearest weeping willow, that willow then wept blood.

The leaves and moss and living matter below, so stained in scarlet, lose their greenery and bleed in a stigmata at once sympathetic and perverse. Roots of the surrounding trees dart away from the afflicted as if unused decades of movement, stored up for a fierce winter that had long been expected yet never endured, are now unleashed in seconds.

The Blood-afflicted willow is shunned and isolated from the whole. Its trunk withers to a blackened, cinder-like husk. The forest is protected.

"Cruelty!" Pestilence screeches.

"Forced suicide of sorts," Death groans.

"They cut off their brethren-sistren," Famine observes. "'Tis cruel indeed. 'Tis unjust, my sister-brothers. Let us seek the heart of this place to do to them what they deserve."

The ways of trees are unknown to most. Given purpose, they will rouse from the torpor of the viridian dream and become deadly sentinels: a curled root for a snare; a broken branch into a trap of spikes; a gnarled knot of bark as a bludgeon. Yet their subtleties are deadlier still: organizing their ranks, army-like, into the impenetrable corridors of labyrinth. The forest alone will permit a traveler to pass – or to become lost.

Bewilderment, unnoticed, entangles the Harbingers' senses. Indeed, imprisoned within Hell's Reprieve they would have had no way of learning the intricacies of a wide, wide world. There was only the cage. There was only stasis. There was only the Beast, unseen down a hallway that led to the antechamber of Hell, who paced away the castoff years under watchful vigil.

But they did learn.

They counted its paces. They noted how the echoes changed in pitch and duration as it slogged eternally around that mysterious entryway. On Earth of yore, cities were founded and crumbled to dust and kingdoms came and went with the wind. But all the while they were learning and eventually they had such a vivid and lucid vision of what lay beyond their reach, it was as though it had been the only thing they had ever seen... and the cage was the illusion.

Tree by tree, a map unfolds between their collective thoughts and their inner unconscious voices start to sense a pattern. They see where Willow Way is trying to lead them, spiraling and looping away from a specific hollow.

One cackles. Then another. And another again until they all share in the darkling mirth of revelation. In celebration of their cleverness, they cast around their magicks and torture indiscriminately flora and fauna alike.

This is the moment the brave fae, ever cautious ever vengeful, unleash an ambush overshadowed only by the epic the skalds sing of their victory at Blightmark March.

Polearms of elm, ensorcelled with poison ivy, streak from the treetops as if shafts of solidified sunlight. The fae who throw them disappear into the trees, avoiding the magicks the Harbingers recklessly fling about in their rage. They shriek, and the noise of it is muffled by choking brush that now grabs them and pulls them down into the dirt.

Words emanate from a towering, elder oak near at hand: "A burial for the ignoble dead."

Thick bark parts into the shape of a smile, a face pushes through with leafy hair, and the body of the fae juts out like a living frieze. This is Laurelai, she who refused a crown for want of freedom and her restless will to roam. Mark her! For she will be important later when Daeli has been broken.

The Harbingers curse her as she dances around them, as she smiles ever wider on inspection of their vine-bound limbs. She cries out, and a second volley of armaments pierce these intruders through and through. The fae emerge from every tree: perched on limbs, hanging from branches, stepping from trunks.

Woe to Laurelai that she misinterpreted their skeletal forms. Not one Harbinger is a corpse for not one has ever lived. Pestilence savors the impotent poison that courses in its veins, that concentrates into its shriveled heart, and finds it a curiosity – not a hindrance.

That same shriveled heart warps the poison, distills it, magnifies it. Striking like an adder bearing fangs, the fingers of Pestilence sink into the vines and expel the antidoteless venom. They wither instantly; the Harbingers rise.

Fae escape, and those will live. But they that, in their fright and haste, merge back into the trees are suffering still. The venom courses from vines to bush to tree, and not even the elder oak can resist. The fae trapped inside scream; their faces appearing on the bark, unable to move.

Fierce Laurelai stands firm, hiding from the Harbingers her leg that is trapped in oak from the knee down.

"You are cursed creatures," she spits. "I know naught from what foul womb you were birthed, nor why you do not die, but there is a grave in this world for every being. Even angels will fall."

The Harbingers advance, weapons raised and spells boiling to the surface of their thoughts. But wise Laurelai counts the number of her days in their steps, grips a branch jutting from the elder oak and pulls out a wooden blade with an edge sharp enough to cleave bone.

And so it does when she swings the edge down, amputating her leg in a single stroke. She stumbles away, gratefully clutching at the branches every unpolluted tree offers: each one a sacrificial crutch that the Harbingers, in bloodlusting pursuit, hack apart.

They will win this chase; bleeding out, she cannot flee. With a hope unformed in her thoughts, she falls against a willow tree, merges into its bark, and is whisked away. She reappears hundreds of miles distant, tumbling out of the edge of the woods and into the human-ruled plains. She fears for the poison her selfish flight has caused, but trusts in the resilience of the forest. Far back, the Harbingers howl in frustration a cry she is too distant to hear.

"The seedling may survive, but this woodland shall rot," Death intones, quelling their wrath.

They progress deeper into Willow Way, where shadows thicken and are friends to none, though the fae ambushers harry their every step. Beyond some imperceptible threshold, these ambushes cease. Quietude descends, blanketing the outskirts of the core of the forest as though a held breath near to suffocation.

The Barrows are here. It is the one place in all the world that the fae dare not tread. All the dead are expelled from the treetops, plummeting into piles of dirt and leaves and needles, to become interred at the whim of the mushrooms that fester, disease-like, on the sodden mulch and loam.

Chips of bone litter the forest floor, glinting even under subdued sunlight. The canopy overhead is near enough a ceiling of a tomb as can be imagined. Though Death finds comfort in this stillness, there is disquiet in its thoughts.

"Be at peace, dear brother-sister," Famine whispers. "Though the denizens in this darkening place may store hostilities in their hearts against us, they will anon glorify themselves with us. You shall see. They are kith."

"And where they are not kith," War echoes, "we shall bend them to our cause."

The life that holds dominion here is now deciding collectively if the track of decomposition on which the Harbingers walk is a carpet lain for the welcome of rulers or a deceptive trap leading to an executioner's chamber. There has ever been a cynical, spiderlike predation in the darkest hollows of Willow Way. I fear, and it may well be, that this indecision is one that hastened the damning of the world. For had the Harbingers been assaulted in force by every being and plant and fungus, the whole of Earth may have united as one against them. Instead, the piecemeal nature of uncoordinated attacks and the pathetic compromise of neutrality in plain sight of purest evil meant some would unite and others would hide, and the price would be everything else.

We sing blessings upon those that resisted, whatever their reasons may have been: they were the first, and so remain foremost in our memories.

Traps indeed await the Harbingers. Each one wounds their pride though fails to mar their broken bodies. These bulwarks do not last; progress is not halted, merely delayed. The venom of Pestilence, that continues to inflict lasting damage on the outer forest, thankfully holds no sway here. As that ichor amused Pestilence before, so too does it amuse the fungus here – and they have already begun to create an antidote, though those efforts will fail anon.

Then, the saprophytes lurch from graves.

It is difficult to describe saprophytes; their forms vary from one to another and shift from circumstance. They are rust and mildew and castoff dregs and fungus, living rotting detritus made in a poor molding. Do they have minds as we? Know they the same feelings that we feel? Only this much can be said with certainty: they appear like shadows made of white flesh and cannot seem to die.

War bisects a saprophyte; it splits in twain, and those two halves renew their attack. Famine crushes another; it collapses inwards, emitting an expulsion of foamy liquid that has the corrosion of acid and a mindless mind to inflict pain. Pestilence gores yet another; its skin bubbles with bubonic sores, then solidifies into scar-tissued armor. And Death cackles all the while, delighting in this brazen defiance:

"Such will to live! Such endless struggle!"

And this fight truly does seem endless. But end it did, though the saprophytes – whether alive and conscious, or not, or neither – have done themselves proud, regardless if pride is something they feel. They bought Daeli, who they did not know and who many yet did not know, the time she needed.

For after waking in her humble home, she had visions. Scattered images that meant nothing then, but everything now. One image above all was lucid: the deteriorated statue of Our Mother-Father, God of All Creation. Its features nigh indistinguishable; Its limbs severed; Its chest riven; Its eyes blinded. Yet, Its mouth smiled. Why? And Daeli asked:

"Why do you smile?"

And a peace descended upon Daeli's heart, and a beam of sunlight descended into her outstretched hands, and she knew the mind of God: *Raise up a holy army, my child.* Daeli went forth. She preached. She sang poetry. She inspired. Few listened, but those that did were faithful. And though she is ignorant of whom her enemies are, her great crusade has momentum the moment Willow Way is murdered.

The second seal is broken.

Lament as I do.
There will be more.
This end is one that creeps.

And so decomposition begins:

> The b e a t i n g heart of woodland
> a pulse loud and constant
> slows, quietens, stills
>   then pumps p a i n f u l l y in reverse.
>   Nourishment does not flow
>   stifled needs, a torment
>   blockage thick and pasty
>   rhizome choking on itself.
> Is this c a n n i b a l i s m
> this defecation so
>   inverted that ceases
>   and cannot expel?
>   Acrid mists rise over r o t t i n g
>   trees the sunlight blanketed
>   roots wormy fleshy spasm
>   in approximation of my ecstasy.

Greenwoods no longer, there is only a poisonous blight. Whatever life persists is frenzied and destroys itself. The Harbingers pass beyond the treeline and never once look back. But what of the civil war they leave behind? Friend devouring friend; the family of light and life uprooted. The fae will not recover from this. Those infected dwell in torment still, and their sistren and brethren who avoid the taint are twisting in despair and seek an absolution that does not exist.

There is an echo here, a sympathetic pain, of Ordeal. And far off: battle cries from demons – bereft of darkness, who burn even at night – as they prey upon the innocent.

Reprobates

The Third Seal

The Harbingers reach the banks of Glassmere. Winds do not speak for fear of carrying these ill tidings further. This is a vigil. It is also an admission of defeat: there are no grand defenders here, set watch by others or of their own volition. And so the air can only caress the stillness of the waters in empathy, in apology for impotent non-intervention.

Pestilence wades in first, relishing the ways in which they can each pervert this exposed sanctum. It reaches out a bony claw, grazes the surface, and motes of pathogens blossom like dandelion pappi. Not even a breeze dares stir, unwilling to be complicit in this widespread, gratuitous genocide. And yet it can do nothing when the magick of Pestilence disperses these motes on gusts of plague:

"Is this not a beautiful sight to behold, brother-sisters, the gentleness that has borne aloft such misery, suffering, and wasting?"

And they all agree in their collective thoughts, shivering in excitement. War enters next, and blood – much of it from the felled fae and butchered saprophytes – leaks out and mixes with the waters until the shallows are ruddy murk. Famine contaminates the rife vegetation, wilted and fragile as wisps of brittle hair, and spreads this enfeeblement down into the deep. Death hardly needs lift a finger; fish and eel and snail and frog alike are all wracked in anguish. But for the deeper things, far below and safe by fathoms, ruin is treading towards them on plodding, inexorable, damned hooves.

Corruption, though potent, does not hold total sway. Inner life, now stirred by horrors, is churning the waters of the lake and diluting the Harbingers' pernicious hatreds. Without a protectress or protector, this is an unconscious and instinctual sacrifice – some will be destroyed earlier, it is so, but the delay brings hope.

And with hope?

Perhaps salvation.

"This display is..." Death's voice rattles to silence.

"Pointless."

"Aberrant."

"Pathetic."

"Useless, yea. 'Tis, sister-brothers, 'tis indeed. But lo, how our ease is undone by our mockery of bodies, these forms in which we have been rough-hewn before—" Death stops, trembling, unwilling to speak Its name. "I say: before we were cast away. Our bones will float; we cannot sink."

And so the heart of the lake is beyond their reach. They explore the strand, venture forth along the shoals to reach rocky islets strewn with scraggly brush. In their passing: a carpeting of death. Yet these deaths grow fewer and fewer, and by and by begin to seem exactly what they masquerade: lashing out at self-fulfilling futility.

Could they simply poison the edges all around and it would prove sufficient? Or might they blast the mighty glacier, all ivory and azure, with their combined magicks until it thickened into dross-filled sputum? And as they scan the horizon, considering foul plans, a screech of outrage pierces their collective minds as all four despair at once.

A mass of clouds drifts languidly by, raining soft rains. In its passing: a carpeting of rebirth. For where each silvery and precious droplet fell, life had sprung anew. The shower subverted all that they had accomplished upon the lake, then floated on its oblivious way. But this is not what truly had aroused their indignation. Now finally turning back and gazing at the paths that they had trod, they spy a patch of blasted Willow Way healed too in spite of its polluted heart.

"We *are* undone!" Death repeats in rage, shaking its scythe at the distancing clouds.

Petty, petulant, the Harbingers plunge their weapons into the waters, release their magicks, to foul the surface yet again. But on high, the clouds continue to float – and float once more they shall above Glassmere.

"There are more forces," Famine relents, "than we had anticipated." Their collective mind noise spikes in denial, then fades to a low buzz of resignation. Isolated for uncounted ages, they had long since become accustomed to rejection and waiting.

Forever awaiting a thing that did not come.

War's voice rumbles, searching for unknown words. Pestilence covers its gaping eye sockets. Death sighs a whisper of emotion, keenly felt by all. And Famine sits, picks up handfuls of earth, and watches as the dirt streams through claws that can only hold weapons, power, and malice.

"We have acted. And praise be that we have, or else our sufferance truly would be eternal. But, dear brother-sisters, let us pause here. Let us truly speak to one another, as we were wont to do because we had nothing," Famine mourns, "except—"

"—each other."

"—suffering in ignorance."

"—tears we could not shed."

Famine bids them join, and each Harbinger sits in turn. "Yea, these things." And then, so encircled, they hold each other's semblance of hands. With a collective discharge of rage, they kindle fire from the weeds that grow between them – weeds that quickly crinkle unto cinders. But the magick flames burn quiet and constant and reassuring.

"Of what shall we speak?" asks War.

It is a question that already contains the answer: the poison and the cure, the curse and the absolution, the end and the beginning. They speak of God, how It damned them for the sin of existence – an existence that God Itself had wrought. As they speak, their mind noise incessantly overwhelms them and they devolve into mad feral animals, weeping and gnashing their teeth.

Only one word pulls them back to lucidity.

Justice.

And I too have wept for them for thinking so. For how could they have ever learned forgiveness when It that made them could not forgive their being? But I have also wept more for God and for the sacrifice It made to atone.

"Already we have cut this world deeply. The mountains hollowing. The forests rotting. The power of It is waning. We will break every seal, have no doubts," Famine decrees.

"Doubts? There can be none," affirms Pestilence. "Our singular focus, however, hath blinded us. 'More forces.' Indeed, ye spake truly, dear sister-brother."

They mull over the events that they had experienced since escaping Hell's Reprieve. The Beast was a formidable opponent and a worthy power all its own. That great battle had sapped the Harbingers of their deepest wells of magick; their hate-filled weaponry, for now, provided a crude crutch to regain such dominance. But it remained to be seen, they admit in low tones, mind noise rising in paroxysms of alarm, if their magick could recover – or if their ebbed tide would continue to ebb until nothing was left and they were powerless before God.

"Haste," Death intones. "We must make haste."

Of the faefolk and saprophytes and the lesser creatures encountered, there was little else to speak: they had fought the Harbingers feverishly, but did not rise beyond the ranks of minor impediments. But what of other kin? At this they balk. What of yet unknown powers?

"I would not have us skulk, brother-sisters," War growls. "'Tis meet that we march, warlike as ourselves, across this land. These thoughts that cow us are but the fetters of It that rejected us. Let us be bold therefore. Power is as power displays, be it true or no."

"And we will know," Pestilence hisses, "what powers there be anon."

"This is well said," Famine stands.

As agitating the surface of the lake had revealed the smallest hint at what unknowns lurked within the deep, so too had their arrival begun to stir the world. Whether they sought knowledge of its dwellers or not, surely in the fullness of time they would learn who had the power to stand against them. And knowing who did not would be equally valuable.

But firm resolve in their underlying thoughts feels flimsy when this insentient lake bests them. Such is the length and breadth of Glassmere that its edges can only be discerned when viewed from the soaring heights, and its great depth is scarcely understood. It is as though they stood on the precipice of a cliff and lacked any ability to plummet despite a compulsion to step forward.

Insight flashes through their collective thoughts. And Death rises, as inevitable as the compulsions that lead all living beings to walk, one day, into its wake. It wades into the waters, concentrates, and strikes a commanding hoof upon the rocky shore.

A single note, cracked and jagged, reverberates downwards at a horrible velocity. This is a knell. This is the origin of an impending sense of doom. Life beneath scatters. One life, fleeting and moribund and suffering, misunderstands the strident noise as a call, a summons, a release from pain.

The afflicted jellyfish bobs to the surface, yearning for relief from a slow wasting. What the poor creature finds instead is the awaiting Harbingers, gurgling in glee with claws extended, who warp and stretch its body in manners both unnatural and grotesque. The resulting violation has the appearance of thinnest, fleshy gossamer ever on the verge of rupturing. But, alas, it endures and the Harbingers enter inside the flensed bubble.

It trembles beneath their hooves. It does not understand. It is in such pain. It feels their mass weighing it down to a place it understands it should not take them. It tries to resist.

And then it obeys.

Sunlight streams downwards, reminding the Harbingers for the briefest moment of the passing clouds – but that light shivers in the undertow of their sinking and dims fathom by fathom unto half-light, like a visual echo. The twisted mass that was a jellyfish quivers, quails, descends into darkness's deepest domain. The day above is snuffed utterly.

Below, a current brushes shadows until they seem to gently beckon: the tops of a submerged forest of seaweed. Bladders filled with gaseous vapors exude random excretions as the Harbingers sink within the depths; turquoise fronds dance about in hypnotic celebrations of gaiety, unknowing of the beings that interrupt their festivities.

In total blackness, phosphorescent algae sparkle starlike along seaweed stalks and mingle with holdfasts rooted into the lakebed. The flesh bubble stops upon the bottom, then rolls farther still towards the lowest nadir where the holdfast of holdfasts is hidden and swallowing secrets.

There are other places in the world hidden from the sight of most mortal kin. Distant reaches where the smallest civilizations, humble yet hoaried by time, eke out existence. The palm gorgons upon the floodplains of Peltan Strand who, in their dreams, survey their terraced fields in moonlit vigils; the tattered wights burrowed within the maw of Sandskrin Vale who wail a nocturne that has not ceased in one hundred years; the ashen men, who are not truly men, atop the last of their strongholds with its gargantuan bronze bell gleaming at dawn. All fall to the onrushing tide of demons that drown, douse, and disperse their remnants in corpse-strewn fields salted with the dead. If this is genocide, it is mindless as it is limitless.

Sobbing on a lonesome hill somewhere cold is Laurelai, hugging a makeshift cane to her chest, as she sees the noxious lavender miasma waft over what was Willow Way. And somewhere else is Daeli, ever marching forward.

The third seal is broken.

Lament as I do.
There will be more.
This end is one that festers.

And so putrefaction begins:

The connective tissue at
once dissolves, slurried
bone-like structures nigh
impenetrable now let go.
They strain to withstand they
reach for mooring lakebed receding until
nothing can resist without and within they let go
of themselves   of each other   of decency.
Exquisite   agony   sinew   churned soft   and
oily   discharge   an   abomination's
ejaculation   dribbles   upwards
to moan   bubbles on the surface.
The filtered spume mixes
my throat clogged
with supplication
vomited   unheard.

What remains of life beneath the surface can no longer be called living. Liquefaction of plant and animal matter was merely its first stage. The dregs recombine, like appendages torn attaching to each other in desperation in the absence of a body. And yet they make of themselves a body of garbage: flowing stagnation of biomass that quivers in the fear of death without the possibility of death, trapped beneath a subsurface of thought unable to form a single one.

This is a child that will never be born. This is a child that will never be aborted. We cannot release it from its horrible birth canal. It is always on the edge of a thing it does not know it cannot grasp. It still cries at night.

The Fourth Seal

All who have eyes now see; all who have ears now hear. Dreadful dawns have risen across the face of a world pockmarked with woe. Where can succor be found? How can the innocent survive? No prophecies have prepared us.

Daybreak through the mountainside, each sunbeam lancing through every hollowed hole. Noontide obscured by patches of toxic mists, thinning only when an errant wind blows out of the east. Twilight reflects off flesh that bulges from spilled embryonic fluids, while the last rays of light – shutting their eyes against monstrosity – dim on the shape of umbilical cord curling out of a cleft in the glacial mass.

There is not metaphor to interpret rightly or wrongly, only a terrible, unforeseen, present reality to witness.

And with a boldness that does not taper, the Harbingers stride into the rolling prairies of Inirnith. The silence that precedes them is as anticlimactic as the silence they leave behind. Humanity has long since known how to hide from the violence of the world. Even the gentle fae have, in times long past, been hostile for reasons that were not entirely just. Every other earthly race has innate powers, both birthright and heritage, and fates that ebb and flow with the seasons.

Yet with wit and cleverness, humans build their own fates with block and beam and forge and fire. Industry becomes them and their industriousness has brokered peace, though some alliances will always remain fraught with tension. Humankind lives in an eternal season of construction and perhaps this is an innate power too, and birthright and heritage, no lesser than the others.

Their weaknesses today are unmistakable as they peek from shuttered windows, cloaks wrapped tight and hoods pulled low as if swaddling themselves and covering their faces will sublimate their forms to transparent smoke. They are foolish because they are bereft. In their hearts, they curse themselves a curse that will come true for rejecting the weird waif who would be warrioress poet and herald divine.

The shivering, huddling humans are indeed fools; the Harbingers do notice them and with an immediacy that would make them blanch – if they knew – as colorless as the flour that powders in their grinding windmills. They notice. And do not care.

Rain clouds have continued to make mockery of their wretched accomplishments, aimlessly drifting hither and yon and staunching wounds and healing scars. With the seals so shattered, these gestures amount to nothing greater than ephemeral kisses upon the foreheads of the dying: gaping holes resolidify in the mountains; poisonous trees recover in the forest; vile putrescence repurifies in the lake. In light of this, what threat humanity? They are dust beneath the Harbingers, who now see threats not in shadows but wheresoever sunlight touches.

Death's voice serrates the silence that travels with them. "There is method in this. There is will."

And yet there is not. The clouds are as much a victim as they, moving on the whims of the wind. But it is true that other powers have arisen from torpors stretching through years nigh uncounted, and will shortly announce themselves with declarations of hostility.

So the Harbingers trudge. Passing farms and fields of wheat, stalks whispering louder than they. Passing hillocks with windmills creaking louder than they. Each fiend has grown so taciturn over the leagues of trodden sweetgrass that their collective mind noise is a barely audible buzz connecting them.

They pass huts and glance at faces staring back – soft and wet like puffy dough with wobbling eyes – then away. And so it happened that they, bleary and disoriented by the endless plains before and behind them, halted their procession not far from the hut of Daeli. Her humble abode is flanked by persimmon trees, the yard grows sweet potatoes, and the front door is wide open: its hinges broken in rapture.

The Harbingers scream and their mind noise spikes to agonizing white noise. Rain showers upon them from the passing cloud cover; their bodies effuse plumes of smoke, each droplet as excruciating as a rusted nail driven into living flesh. When the clouds have moved on, all four fiends remain writhing on the ground and clawing for a path out of the puddles left behind.

"Damn the sky! I spit at its divinity!" Pestilence cries out. "How dare it raise up arms against us!"

It is a pathetic sight that such a meagre thing casts the Harbingers so low. Of this they are fully aware, but will not make mention of it even in the undercurrent of their thoughts. It is repulsive indeed, this shame.

"Would that I could rake these clouds," War bellows, "into ragged strips of skin."

"Vigilance, sister-brothers," Famine sobs. "Let us be aware of the comings and goings of this enemy. When its course is clear, we must seek shelter."

"Or else cloak ourselves," Death groans, "in borrowed skins."

They had never before had need to cover the wreckage of their bodies for there was little there, and they did not know that they were naked. What a queer sight, then, to see these figures with contorted arrangements of bone wading through tall grass, seeking the tattered linens of the poor left on lines to dry. What a sad sight, later, to see these figures struggle and fail to drape improvised hoods over their heads because of the horns that protrude from their skulls.

And what fearful, naive confusion is felt by the humans that watch them do these things. These peasants who, from tradition and the oral histories of their grandsires that lived to see and survive such bloody days, place offerings at their doorsteps on the porches of their homes: tart apples, baked breads, candied nuts, and dried meats.

The Harbingers do not notice.

And I pity them for this: they do not even understand what food is, nor what such a gesture could mean.

Now is the rainy season and the clouds pass often by. The Harbingers flee at the sight of white soaring upon the horizon, shiver and huddle together around conjured fires at the base of abandoned windmills and within earthen caves and under lonely copses, and they come to know new pains nursed by the rejection of God that never fully evaporates from their collective thoughts.

At times, they strike out with their powers to test the land, to find weaknesses, to alter the terrain to lessen their burden. But these experiments backfire and do little to aid and much to harm their progress. The path to the heart of these plains is arduous, and the fields that extend in all directions in unvaried colors and unvaried cadences remind them of the horror of eternity.

"It is as if," Death murmurs, "a new cage."

And yet they learn, as ever. Unthreatened by humanity, even the grandiose castles that watch them come and go as they trek through the grasslands, they can hear the whispers of the peasants and the merchants and the rulers: Daeli the Lightbringer, Daeli the Scorned, Daeli the Hermaphrodite.

Most speak of the latter with voices sopping in spite and disgust: of the stupid child, who had barely begun to bleed, with delusions of God of All Creation choosing it as an avatar against the coming night; of the aberrant child, whose cracking voice had neither the softness of a girl nor the hardness of a boy, with both the genitalia of a woman and a man; of the mad child who, after preaching fanciful stories in the gutters of the streets, marched away with a multitude of the best and strongest among them and left those that would not heed her words of warning far behind.

And to hear these things thrilled the Harbingers until the dreariness that afflicted them had abated. A hermaphrodite! A creature cursed to be neither! A non-entity!

"Are we not strangely blessed?" Famine mocks.

"Yea, sister-brother, it is so," chimes Pestilence. "For we have no superfluousness and are thusly whole. Rejoice!"

And they do. And their celebration – offensive as it is, petty and childish in its yearning to aggrandize the emptiness inside – is misunderstood by the men and women that hear it, who believe: the storm is passing, the storm is passed, the clouds will part to reveal the sunlight once again. They believe, so firmly, these mistruths of which they have convinced themselves to such a certitude that they are as blind and ignorant as the Harbingers themselves.

Woe is coming, and the rejection of Daeli haunts hollowed hearts still. Even her forgiveness cannot refill this famished void.

Deeper into the fields the Harbingers tramp, until sunflowers tower over them with heavy-lidded, watchful eyes. An unnatural metallic glint appears between the stalks as a gentle breeze brushes by – and then careens forward and slams into the Harbingers with perilous impact, dividing them from each other. Here is an abnormal manufactured being, the only creation that God did not create.

Scarecrows, made of mechanical know-how and minor enchantments. It is these, the smallest and least sentient of magicks, that cause the half-straw and half-steel automatons to assault the Harbingers. Not since the fae of Willow Way have they met such resolve. But while the fearlessness of the scarecrows matches that of the saprophytes, they are not wholly mindless; they mark the Harbingers for what they are: interlopers that threaten the crops.

Each Harbinger, for the first time, fights alone. Their distance from one another is such that their mind noise is stretched towards the point of snapping and their collective thoughts are splitting. They cast spells, blighting the ground and brush and sunflowers, yet none affect the scarecrows who fall upon them with passionless hate.

It is a disorienting assault on their bodies and more so on their minds. They feel something they have barely ever acknowledged: a welling individuality. It is loathsome and terrifying and feels like a second damnation of sorts.

Pure isolation.

On instinct, they rely on the keen edge of their weaponry and strike out with animalistic savagery. Without magick, without coordination, pell-mell chaos becomes a creeping battle of attrition with no way of knowing who is winning. Every scarecrow's worldview narrows until a single Harbinger is the only thing in all of existence. And their numbers continue swelling. Famine falters; Pestilence trips; War stumbles; Death falls.

Yet they, baleful and blind of all things save desperation, inch by inch return to themselves. Clarity of purpose. The stakes of their grand plans. Pain eternal and shared suffering. And high above it all, beyond cloud and sky and sun and star, a distant hope so remote and minute as to seem unattainable. Freedom eternal and shared salvation.

Daeli seeks the same in her own way, though she is unconscious of it. Her army swells with song and sings homilies in the form of her poetry. Wherever they go, their vision of her inflates and they claim – to the creatures met on their march – that she performs miracles. But she does not. That time will come later. Today she scours the known and forgotten reaches of the world for equally known and forgotten relics. She dons these holy artifacts and burnishes herself in the blessings of God. She is shining! Praise be.

But as she digs in graveyards, searches mausoleums by torchlight, stalks the halls of catacombs with her face as grim as the countless dead that watch her fade from sight, the demonic tide has broken and rolls backwards towards Ordeal. Their scattered forces somehow manage to find the ageless watchers in their hovels of bracken, and slaughter them while they sleep; each death is a library lost forever.

The fourth seal is broken.

Lament as I do.
There will be more.
This end is one that smolders.
And so degradation begins:

Smokeless fire licking at the blades
of grass taking flight
unrooted, rooted in hysteria
spread a kindled chain reaction.
The windmills ignite
spinning wheels
shriek ember tears
watering ground now inert.
Wind itself is milled into hymnals
unholy verses unholier
chorus darkling glory
amidst the soul.
Fields harrowed by a sickness
reap a harvest of anguish
and the winnowed chaff that tingle my fingers
as they drop to the ground like leper's alms.

There is only madness here. The winds that once graced the fields to the sweetest susurruses have fled; in their absence, usurping their rule: gibbering squalls and laughter. It is a pale imitation of the laughter the Harbingers emitted in mock of Daeli, but more frightening as it erupts from human throats throughout the kingdom of Inirnith.

Those who believed in her words and had faith retain their minds. Woe unto them. For it was only ailment, age, and disability that kept them from marching by her side and now, overwhelmed by the bizarre noises of their kin, they too become mad and many, the instant before succumbing, commit suicide in the most horrifying manners imaginable.

Reprobates

The Fifth Seal

Balance tips. The Harbingers of the Apocalypse wax; God of All Creation wanes. There are no words to describe this horror adequately, and so there will be none when worse comes to pass. And it is coming soon; the interconnected foundations of the world quake and reality unravels, as though knitting needles puncture fabric and yank in opposite directions. Creation will be undone.

Daeli's Crusade is illuminated like a chorus of angels. She finds new recruits, but never enough; she glances over her shoulder and sees destruction rising from her homeland, and hastens her steps. She cannot yet return. There remain buried secrets, stories out of the living past half-remembered in an era of peace, that she must uncover.

Laurelai is alone. Lost in a broken land, lost in herself, within regrets and traumas and memories and fantasies she seeks for companionship and finds only herself: only her voice speaking to her own ears; only her ears hearing her own words; only her eyes seeing her own hollow face; and only her face witnessing eyes hollowing hollower still. She is become a puppet with none to move her towards action. Trapped in herself, she is trapped in despair. And when she walks, she does not know where she is going.

Some pockets of humanity persist in the world. I write this in tribute to them for they cannot: their yoke is too heavy and there is too much to be done. And yet they survive when others have not and render aid where others do not; hope is not lost in their hearts and so they will always abide forever in mine.

The Harbingers turn away from what humans yet endure in the scorched plains. Any huddled masses they encounter, they ignore and walk on by. The blasted prairie is fully behind them and the huts that stipple the fields disappear beneath the weight of horizon. Grass transitions to scrub, and then to barren wastes, and then to xeric lands where the very air is drier than the sand. And so they enter Kharhoom.

There is a desolation here unknown to the rest of the world. Its emptiness cannot be called peaceful; soaked into the sands, trickling deep down into aquifers that have been empty for aeons, are the histories of many people who are neither missed nor remembered. This is an old place; its true story is a codex with more pages than the rest of creation combined. And at the end of the age, when all is dust, still it will dwarf whatever else occurs in the flowing and ebbing stories and fortunes – good and ill – of every other living being.

But of the beings that came before and did deeds in these harsh lands, I will say no more. For I do not know, and some things are better left unsaid and some pains untouched.

The Harbingers, very strangely, may intuit some of it. As they gaze upon all that they can see, familiar feelings scrape at them from the inside. Kharhoom. Hell's Reprieve. Neither are connected in any way, tangible or otherwise, but the ambience must possess an edge as keen as their scythes because they balk. Their hooves sink into the shimmering, metallic sands and tremble.

"Come away, brother-sisters," one states. "We go."

And yet they do not move. And they do not know who spoke. And the power they have acquired suddenly means nothing. And they look up and see the expanse of sky, azure with a blazing white orb hung at the very zenith, and the wind picks up and brushes their broken bodies and finds gaps in their shrouds and makes their bones sigh and passes through them, shivering the sands. And the dunes release a booming chorus of supernal grace and glory, and then it stops and passes away.

Such silence. For a time, they hold hands with one another while their mind noise is uneven and uncertain. The dunes continue to shift, their coloration and mottled patterns unremittingly changing: bronze, silver, gold, and platinum; brass, copper, iron, and lead. Windblown, eternal mandalas.

But there can be respite neither for such as these or for any others while such as these stalk the surface of creation. Time prods them onwards, while capricious clouds beyond their sight are healing the wounds they rent into the world. In a time of action, be it violent or remedial, there is no second to pause for breath. The turn has come; we must go on.

Demons know this lesson well: the drums of warfare are their beating hearts; the blood of victims is the sweat that streaks their flesh. Rest is anathema; sleep unknown, save for the halcyon age they spent in the subterranean caverns that veined the roots of Ordeal. In that blind darkness they discovered a new way forward apart from conquest, rage perpetual, and wanton strife. Mining, architecture, art. An unexpected and unplanned renaissance of mind and spirit. The edge of transcendence was yet in reach the moment the Harbingers, in ignorance and apathy, forced the demonic race back onto the only path they had ever trod.

The tide of subjugation returns, flows through the ruin of their home beneath Ordeal and out into Willow Way and Glassmere and Inirnith and the unnamed spaces in between. They are no longer an organized legion; scattered and spread thin, they are roving bands and pairs and singletons who prey indiscriminately upon anyone not in hiding.

Some – the most bloodthirsty – broke away from the legion and chased the sunset until they had circumnavigated the world. Such wonders they saw; such slaughter they left behind for sunrises to rebehold day after day. And so it came to pass that a hecatomb of corpses brought them to the other side of Kharhoom, where they wandered about in disarray until they spied the Harbingers entranced in a nightmarish, dazed reverie.

Battle is joined. Ore-scooping shovels, turned crude halberds, crash against scythes; lode-piercing pickaxes, turned crude warhammers, slam into snaths. The ferocity of each strike is like a lure, calling more demons to the clash.

This is the first time the Harbingers fight something akin to an equal. The demons use blistering magick that, while lacking the grace and potency of the Harbingers' sorcery, possesses a raw, irresistible intensity; such atavistic carnage forces any offensive counterattack to immediately pivot to the defensive, and then that defense buckles.

It is true that the younger and newer generations have not lived through the terrors their ancestors visited upon the world. There are no survivors, demonic or angelic, who can recount firsthand the Sacking of Sehvront after the final betrayal, or the gloaming that preceded the Battle of Zyx, or the Endless Siege of Glory Hill that lasted three decades, or even the First and Second Miseries where peace was left twitching on the floor of the emptied council chamber. But the impulses that drove their forebearers are as alive in them now as they ever were in antiquity.

Were Kharhoom not so remote or, at the very least, inhabited by any civilization that could have observed the melee, the Harbingers might have been stopped. The demons, if they could not best them, would have become an unwitting bulwark against the cataclysm. If they had held out longer, hindered the Harbingers further, Daeli Lightbringer would have returned in triumph and ended the threat. This book of suffering would have been closed and sealed for all time; instead, the page was simply turned.

The conclusion of this confrontation feels predestined; like so much that has been and so much that will yet be, there is only pain and unpreventable loss. Gray blood oozes across the dunes like the brush strokes of a deranged artist. The demonic ichor smokes, then ignites in the dying rays of the sun. By nightfall, it will be subsumed under sand. By dawn, no trace will endure and the only proof of its existence will be in the shadows left by my clumsy words.

Sin does not end this day. It haunts a lifeless corner of the world, prowling through the ever-shifting maze of dunes.

The desert's heart is difficult for the Harbingers to locate. Metallic, crystalline fulgurites jut from the gibber plains as if petrified flowers that lost hope in long days gone; these emit a disorienting energy that rebounds against near and distant outcroppings, then echoes plaintively until their senses are entirely confounded.

For a demon or human or fae, or any other kin, nothing of the sort would occur. Such as those would only suffer the unbearable heat, arid conditions, and lack of sustenance. The crystals would be a passing fancy. But whereas the collective thoughts of the Harbingers were nearly severed amid the sunflower fields of Inirnith, here their mind noise becomes a hissing clamor devoid of intent, meaning, and understanding. It exists as a featureless plateau that wraps in upon itself from all angles without any edge off of which one could escape.

"We are—"

        "Breaking—"

"Forward and—"

      "Not backward—"

"Sisters—"

"Brothers—"

     "Who are—"

"We now?"

Trapped in a desert of their own minds without the oasis of a soul. The sight is pitiful. If only the demons had fallen upon them now. The Harbingers clutch each other as crutches, now pressing their skulls together like hands in supplication, to the point of physical agony, in their need for connection. Fear is the only sensation they share. And though they are unable to form the thoughts clearly, they are not oblivious to the need to break through this dire threat.

"We must risk—" Death chokes. "Losing ourselves." And with a primal cry, it pushes the others away. "Flee, brother-sisters—" And now using its scythe as a cane and staggering off. "Disperse and flee from ourselves!"

37

And the Harbingers flee. Their fear has been embodied within themselves and relief only comes when they are far from one another. But it is a sickening relief when they look back across distances and realize how far they ran, how small they appear, how detached they are. There is a shame. In that moment if they had internal organs, surely they would have vomited.

"Does my voice reach?" Famine asks, but it sounds as though a reed whispering thinly in the wind.

"It does reach," War responds, also as a whisper without its normal solid substance.

"We have not been defeated by this," Pestilence calls, its timbre like a faint echo of an echo. "Be heartened, dear my sister-brothers. Listen! Though we speak over a gap between us, yet we can coordinate. Let us go forthwith and finish this thing."

Their progress is halting and wends through rough terrain surrounded at irregular intervals by eroded bluffs, dunes, and the peculiar and hateful crystals that amplify their mind noise yet threaten their collective thoughts. And then, on the horizon, a mass of clouds drifts towards them. To this enemy, they turn their full attention and ire. And they plan. And they wait.

But Daeli hurries onward. Anxiety fills her; she is like a vessel that is on the verge of overflowing – one that contains more than it should; each passing hour is another drop of heavy liquid. Within a city of old death, within a crumbling crypt, within a columbarium full to bursting as she, there is a cenotaph and not the grave she expected. She recalls her vision: a sunbeam descended into her outstretched palms and she felt its warmth, but not its heat, and a wholeness encircled her. There was a peace unlike any she had ever known. But now she feels only disquiet, and does not know where this holy weapon hides, so she prays.

God is silent.

The fifth seal is broken.

Lament as I do.
There will be more.
This end is one that blasphemes.

And so vitrification begins:

*Sands
scorching
hazy air
to liquid.
Aloft the clouds are ignorant
merrily approaching torturous death, rains
that will become tears first for themselves then
for someone else then for no one.
Melted metals
twisting upwards
into threads of
depraved glass.
A phurba
pinioning
my lungs with
serrated breaths.*

A gleaming spire of perversion pierces into the sky, towering over even the highest peak of Ordeal, and pins the mass of clouds in place so it can no longer move. And yet unseen and more horrible still, this filth penetrates as deeply into the Earth as high as it soars. This is the second rape! There will be one more! The core of the world shudders.

Can it be said the Harbingers are capable of experiencing true joy? Or is this profane display of unrepressed jubilation simply a physical reflex? Their paroxysms are so intense and crass that they appear as seizures. Yet they cry out as any stricken, innocent child would once a prolonged period of sickness and duress had finally ended.

Reprobates

The Sixth Seal

Others will call it petty revenge, some will say curiosity, more will understand that the Harbingers knew exactly what they were doing even in their collective deaf-blindness. The urge to kill is as instinctual as it is premeditated in those that commit to the course of murder.

As the whole of Kharhoom melted and bubbled, they strained to mold the uncontrollable powers it released into weaponized spite. In this they succeeded and now, dancing around raindrops that impotently dribble into smooth basins trenching what was a desert, they reach the base of the gargantuan, glassy spike that spears the clouds.

The surface shatters into webworked cracks under their hooves, creating vulgar stairs for their perverse ascent. This foreshadowing is unmistakable and a tragedy in itself. It is fitting then, but no less heart-rending, that they summit the lowest bank of clouds at the start of sunset. Woe, for the sun will rise no more on what it once quietly illumed an epoch.

Here there are angels. Generations in seraphic glory who, unbeknownst to the whole of the world below, live and love and multiply in peaceful grief. But these are not the shunned angels of millennia past, the third of the heavenly host that chose exile from God of All Creation's realm in order to war upon the demons that threatened the existence of every other mortal kin; the Fallen have long since faded from glory, they have been smothered beneath the pages of history, and any who survive are surely pale shades of what they had once been. Nay, these are the angels who stayed – the loving choir that God Itself expelled for reasons they do not know and never shall.

Even now, gazing backwards, I do not fully comprehend the reason myself and I fear that, if I did, it would break my heart as eternally as it has theirs. And so, they tended the world as though a garden, and nurtured it to blooming in hopes that it would please Its sight and bring joy unending to Its heart. Their devotion moves me to this day.

But the divine absence, in spite of their fidelity, cut them deeply and in ways they were incapable of realizing until the Harbingers violated the sanctity of their only home-in-exile. If the Fallen were shadows, the Faithful were vacant dolls.

A multitude gazes heavenwards, rapt by the sudden sight of the spire in their midst; some stroke it tenderly, some extend fingertips in the direction of its pinnacle – towards the sun. All believe, so ardently and dutifully, that this is a sign from God: an intercession, an omen, the end of their long sadness. They cannot sense the looming threat.

Alas for the angels. In cruel ways, this is indeed an intercession and an omen and the end of their long sadness. The Harbingers can feel the weak and pulsating heart of Nimbus-the-Kingdom-of-Cloud high up in the cirro expanse.

"Foolish were they to provoke us, my brother-sisters," War croons. "For I knew naught, until this very instant, that another seal was hidden in this place."

"Nor I," the rest cackle in premature triumph, basking in a reconnection with each other that feels stronger and more enduring than ever it was before trekking into the wastes.

Of the first battle in the sky, there is little to tell. It is slaughter. An age has passed since the last spilling of holy blood; such a precious thing should not occur so lightly nor go so unnoticed. A chorus of lamentation should echo from out of the firmament and resonate into the cavernous chambers of the Earth for a single droplet shed. Instead, in silence, there is unceremonious deluge. O humanity! Do you not mourn the loss now? Do you not yet weep for those that died in ignorance for thee? Daeli will. She who is the Lightbringer will sit beside those who suffered the trauma of this night, those whose trauma surfaces at every gloaming, those to whom trauma makes every dying sun another death that they relive again. She will hold their hands. She will wipe away every tear from their eyes. She will try to comfort. But they will know the first things have passed away.

Though fixed in the sky, the clouds begin churning into patterns that rearrange the order of the lofty dwellings and corridors and towers that fill the kingdom. Archangels see the dead and dying and arm themselves with blessed spears and clad themselves in gleaming armor and go to war for the very first time in their history of peace. As below, so above: the Faithful join a battle of necessity for the preservation of good as the Fallen had once waged. Connected in spirit across millennia, these angels finally understand at once the compelling emotions that moved their sistren to action. And in their hearts: empathy, forgiveness, and love.

A clarion call, like a trumpet at the break dawn, resounds from the newly-formed barbican of cumulus. There stands, erect and ready, the luminous figure of Grace-from-Glory as she cries aloud a sonorous note from her marmoreal throat to muster the heavenly host. Songs of hallelujah rain down from the sunglow-tinged nimbus overhead.

"Glory to God of All Creation in the Highest Heaven! And Peace to Its People on Earth!" the angels sing.

"Gloria!" Grace-from-Glory chants.

"Gloria!" the archangels repeat, standing beside her now atop the battlements, with spears aloft.

"Lord of All Light, who takes away the Sins of the World, have Mercy on them!" the angels sing.

"Kyrie!" Grace-from-Glory chants.

"Kyrie!" the archangels repeat, appearing between the crenelations along the ramparts and upon turrets flanking the parapet, with arrows nocked and quivers full.

"Mother-Father of All Children, who finds the Lost and leads them Home, grant them Peace!" the angels sing.

"Amen!" Grace-from-Glory chants.

"Amen!" the archangels repeat.

"Amen…" the angels throughout Cloud Kingdom pray, softly and hopefully and devoutly, in countless whispers united into the unyielding force of eternity.

And the Harbingers clap their claws together mockingly, clatter their jaws in mirth, stamp their hooves in uncertain cadences, and shrilly attempt to repeat some of the phrases, but recite them all incorrectly. Their offensive foolishness reveals a more profound incompetence: the rage of the demons in the desert – in its violent simplicity – is a thing the Harbingers fathom; the compassion of the angels in the clouds – who pray for their peace and not their deaths – is wholly unfathomable.

"Lay we siege, sister-brothers mine?" Pestilence asks.

"Yea, until the walls come tumbling down," War states.

The warrior archangels are not prepared fully for the polluted magicks the Harbingers unleash. Doom disperses cloud cover into evaporated steam that scalds their skin; Plague slinks over the ground, covering their feet with buboes; Wither creeps into their bones, finding flaws and widening them unto cracking; Blood boils the life essence flowing in their veins until their hearts roast inside their chests, and they die in agony clutching uselessly at nothing.

Yet they endure. The restructuring of the clouds into this tiered stronghold is surely the best the angels could have done; it slows the unabated assault drastically. However, the unholy spike that stabbed their domain through and through sapped the kingdom's powers and only allowed a single reformation. This configuration is a gamble, as are often the most important choices in life.

Under time and pressure, the battlements do indeed begin to crumble as War had decreed: new pathways broken into the ramparts through which they press their attack.

"We remain steadfast!" Grace-from-Glory cries out.

And her words are as true as the miracles the archangels perform: dividing the last arrow in their quivers into many, until their quivers are full once more; turning rainwater into viscous honey, retarding the Harbingers' climb and inflicting excruciating pain; healing the wounded; raising the dead.

Even the young cherubim, most incapable and innocent, find ways to become useful without prompting or orders. Those elder seraphim that cannot be cured of affliction they carry away, gripping the bodies as a flock and flying into the unreachable heights; here they set up a field hospital, easing suffering with bandages soaked in holy water and offering tender smiles. And when the weapons of the warriors shatter under onslaught, they soar down with replacements and buoy the spirits of their protectresses with hymns of thanksgiving and lovingkindness.

On another day in another place when the sun has truly set in her heart, Grace-from-Glory will also sing this song to console herself – and then, much later, as a rallying cry in times of hopelessness.

Onwards through the trials
of everlasting pain
towards an ever-rising dawn
and then, at last, to gain
Understanding and Love
of Thee Divine,
who hears my soul's
fracturing under life's unending time.

Onwards past the gloom
of gloaming twilights gone
towards an ever-shining sun
and then, at last, a home
built and filled with Riches
of Thy Care Divine,
who soothes my soul's
wounds and unburdens all my mind.

Praise to Thee, O Creator! Glory to Thy Good!
My spirit sings: Thou Art! My joy too deep for words!

Onward the battle rages. Through the barbican, through terraces turned parapets, throughout a keep that had been a temple echoing with canticles from dawn to dusk yet now echoing with scythes against spears, and bloodlet screams. Now out into gardens become bulwarks, higher, higher, over moats, past pinnacles, higher still, beyond waterfalls and shrines and homes that soon will lay empty as unfilled graves, underneath nimbus tinged with thickening crimson.

There are less and less archangels to hold the Harbingers at bay. Miracles are more difficult to perform and their effects diminish. The light is fading fast and the heart of Nimbus-the-Kingdom-of-Cloud is visible across the stratus. The Harbingers gather themselves and combine their magicks together in new and devastating combinations that blast out in force more the sum of their parts.

So many cherubim beg Grace-from-Glory to flee with them into the heights; she is injured worse than anyone, yet fights off the loving hand of each cherub that attempts to lay hold of her. They have stopped singing. They are sobbing. They do not understand her desperation because they do not understand the consequences of loss. They have lived so little, they only know of Heaven from stories, and so they cannot see how the present becomes the future nor why it must be fought for so fiercely.

Grace-from-Glory fights for them, but they do not know it. In their blessed innocence, they simply see her dying again and again only to resurrect more painfully each time, to suck in more rarified air as if it is a final breath, to death rattle on her back with her wings pinned and twitching behind her shoulders as she watches – through glazing eyes – the nimbus above tinging with lavender lividity.

She cannot stop; she must endure. And the last time she dies she tries to pray, but forgets the words. She hums instead God's favorite hymn as the growing winds deafen her. Cirrus stretches. Noctilucent clouds waver. Night falls.

The sixth seal is broken.

Lament as I do.
There will be more.
This end is one that darkens.

And so dissolution begins:

Black bulbous pall stippled
pink as flushed skin
flashing with lightning
wadded tight as bandages.
Filaments extend up
disdain into celestial aether
tenebrous trembling
a link to a star.
Plucked as music foul
singleton note
unheeded by mortals
echoes of doom.
It abscises forever the
sinews of my arms
reaching for candles
coldly snuffed.

Midnight grows colder and darker by degrees as each star is blotted from existence one by one. The angelic choir is no more; the survivors of the siege lose their inner song, and their grief is no longer peaceful. Baleful electricity arcs between torn clouds, revealing empty stares and minds overcome by a repeated refrain: they have lost their home for a second time. And the miracle of flight is rescinded.

Injured seraphim stay, unable to move or be reached. Fledgling cherubim plummet from the sky. And archangels float wherever the wind wills, and are never seen again. But this same wind, far below, is exhorting countless unfurled banners with the symbol of a sun. Daeli has returned.

Reprobates

The Seventh Seal

Sunrise at the edge of the known world. The horizon is the color of yellow poppies. The breeze smells of harvested wheat. There are the sounds of whispered oaths, and words of faith and camaraderie, and all the good things that dwell deep in the hearts of every human being. Although she has been fasting, on Daeli's tongue is the taste of persimmons and sweet potatoes and something else that defies description.

Morning light infuses her. Her copper skin glistens from sweat and dew. Her rough-chopped hair is as auburn as the fields of her homeland. Of late there has been an urgency in her hazel eyes, but now they are placid; she has done all she can. Only her faith can lead her the rest of the way, as it has from out her front door to the base of this lopsided hill.

Dawn is her hour. She has been awake all night waiting for its coming: sharpening her sword; polishing her armor; touring the bivouac; sitting with the watch; treading softly from tent to tent while exchanging kind and quiet words to those – like her – who cannot sleep. And when they ask if she will pray with them: she smiles, takes them by the hand, bows her head and closes her eyes, and offers up some words to God and calls them by their names.

Daeli's Crusade stands ready, her army now assembled. But they do not know the horrors that hide over the horizon. They cannot see the perforation of Ordeal, the murk choking Willow Way, the pollution of Glassmere, the smoke blanketing Inirnith, the liquified Kharhoom, or immobilized Cloud Kingdom hanging like a corpse on a pike left to rot.

Nor can Daeli see this, who feels growing resolution, as she dreams of tomorrow spent in commune with her God. Turning her back on all she had known, she marched into the great unknown and found herself here. She always wondered what the future would bring.

It brings death and pestilence and famine and war in the shape of four shadows treading across that obscured horizon without hesitation, heading straight for her.

The ranks of the Crusade are rigid. Daeli is before them, gleaming like a morning star. From the humblest beginnings to an avatar of light; from a ragtag crowd to a swelling mass of believers. She raises her battle standard and it catches the rays of the sun. Her Crusade makes a joyful noise.

"Daeli the Lightbringer! Child of God!" they shout.

She plants the bright banner into the willing earth. And unsheathing her sword, raising it like a noontide sunbeam, she lifts her voice and leads her army in martial song.

> *God, our blessed friend,*
> *leads us 'gainst the foe;*
> *Forward into battle joined,*
> *see our banner go!*

> *At Thy sign of triumph*
> *Hell's doomed host doth flee;*
> *On, then, children of the Lord:*
> *on to victory!*

> *Evil's foundation quivers,*
> *trod 'neath our many feet;*
> *God, our blessed parent,*
> *protects us from defeat.*

> *Glory, laud, and honor*
> *unto Thy charity;*
> *Sing we now our praises:*
> *on to victory!*

A wave of glowing light appears to flow behind Daeli as each crusader takes their assigned place in formation. Silence descends. The only sound is the coming of the Harbingers: their hooves striking the ground with drum-like inevitability; their snaths cracking rocks wherever they land.

Unimpressed, unthreatened, unhindered, all four walk by the whole host of gathered humanity and the juvenile who led them. They continue up the hill, climbing towards a thing only they perceive. In their collective thoughts: their one true foe, a battle to be joined, triumph, victory; all glory, laud and honor unto themselves.

Daeli breaks away from her army and interjects herself between the Harbingers and their goal. When they begin to tread around her, she thrusts her sword at their black hearts.

"Fiends of the underworld, stand and be judged! Thou art cursed and rejected by the world! I charge thee, before God Itself, stand and be judged!"

The Harbingers rouse from their dazed stupor.

"What speaks this one of *judgement*?"

"We have already been *judged*."

"Yea! We now go to the *trial*!"

"'Tis most meet that we now—"

"Render a *sentence*," they intone in unison.

And, gazing down upon Daeli Lightbringer for the first time, they recognize her from everything they had overheard and fall upon themselves in cruel laughter.

"What *is* it?" Famine asks.

"A *thing*!" Death responds.

"The thing *speaks*!" War exclaims.

"What does *it* say?" Pestilence wonders.

"*Nothing that it understands*," they shout in unison.

And, gazing up at the Harbingers of the Apocalypse in fear for the first time, Daeli at last comprehends the nature of the enemy her God had sent her to slay. They knock her dull sword from her grip, they strike her armor from her body, they tear the clothing away that covers her modesty and laugh crueler laughs still. They raise her body up, as though a toy, displaying her to each other and making mock of the dual genitalia, her hermaphroditic nature revealed.

"Behold the woman-man!" they cackle in glee.

There are some who call this incident Daeli's Shame. I do not countenance this, but I inscribe it here in order to refute. This was not the Shame of Daeli, for there was nothing the Harbingers could say of her that she had not already thought herself. As they bandy her about, pointing at her groin and amusing themselves with the hot tears that streak her trembling face, she can only hear her own words echoing back from across time every memory when she asked, staring at her reflection for another countless moment,

... what am I?

And so the Harbingers answer her question many years hence at a place she did not intend to go while doing a thing she did not intend to do:

"Small is the worth of the girl-boy named Daeli!"

They set her down. And they leave, stalking up the weedy hillside and away. And of the Crusade? Nothing. Demoralized, they too leave. Daeli does not give up. She covers herself; she hurries back to them; she speaks of the evil the Harbingers represent and the need – in this, the hour of their great need – to strike them down and return them whence they came. But the Crusade is truly over. Even when, heads lowered in despair and disgust, they drop their weapons to the ground and Daeli rushes to them and takes up their weapons and puts them back in their hands, one by one, over and over, they drop their weapons again, and they leave. The Crusade is over. It is done.

Witness Laurelai witnessing Daeli in defeat: she has crested the hillside, herself long emptied of tears, and with unbesmirched clarity watches the army disperse. But she sees the Lightbringer and feels only hope. War passes by, and yet she feels hope. Famine passes by, and yet she feels hope. Pestilence passes by, and yet she feels hope. Death passes by, and yet she feels hope.

And a love that surpasses all understanding keeps her heart and mind through Daeli Lightbringer, Child of God.

Within the Harbingers, however, there is an unexpected kind of shame. Their mind noise is the most dissonant it has ever been, but they do not know why. As Daeli's piercing voice, words unintelligible over the din of wordless thought, cries unto the heavens above, they bury their confusion along with the blades of their scythes into the hilltop.

Blood embraces Wither; Wither wraps with Doom; Doom coils about War; War infuses Plague; and every other wicked permutated pair joins itself with its sibling sin and transmutes into the penultimate blasphemy against all life, the world, and creation.

This rape is the third! There will be worse hereafter! A gaping hole is torn through reality and a Gate of Heaven – which should not exist – is pulled against its will into being. The Harbingers commit sacrilege by stepping over the threshold and placing their hooves upon the ivory stones beyond. From this point on, each step they take is a greater profanity and a desecration that can never be washed away.

The Gate collapses behind them, barring entrance of any who would dare oppose the Harbingers. But this is merely an abscess over an infection that has no cure; the divine realm is attempting to contain contagion that cannot be contained.

Their mind noise is as silent as the grave. They are, it is strange to write, in awe of Heaven. Despite themselves and the ill intent that bore them here, they are overwhelmed by the sight of that which they were never meant to see: towering marble columns and roofs of purest alabaster, all etched in looping patterns of orichalcum; streets of ivory lain with care; empty terraces and verandas and courtyards and homes, filled with musical instruments that lay abandoned upon the ground; the sky, an eternal noon without a sun; flowers everywhere, a rainbow in every bouquet; and peace that is tangible and cannot be further described.

These wonders lead to a door barred from the inside past which is the holy of holies, Highest Heaven.

The Harbingers break wide the groaning door. And there it waits alone: the vacant Throne of God. Seven steps below, sprouting from the floor, stands a massive cross upon whose form is crucified God of All Creation. O Mother-Father, dearest Lord, why – oh why – were you there? Why were you hoisted so pitiably with three pearlescent nails the size of obelisks penetrating each of your wrists and both your ankles? And why did you not struggle against your pains?

None of these questions enter the minds of those fiends who are now overcome with hatred. They all cry out at once, speaking over one another yet saying the exact same words.

"Why wouldst thou damn us, who had never known life? Why wouldst thou confine us, who had never done harm? Predestined to Hell before the hour of our birth! Alone! Scorned! Unwanted! Are we not thy children as well as they, the tiny beings that scurry and stumble on that wide world hewn by thy hands? Speak, then, of our true iniquities! Why dost thou reject us before we knew thy loving touch?"

Tears the size of boulders drop from the blindfold bound around God's eyes. They cleanse the floor, but drown the Harbingers in harrowing torments. Death and Pestilence and Famine and War shriek, then lash out with vengeful strokes of their unholy scythes, piercing the pure skin of God, and flooding Highest Heaven with consecrated blood.

"Holy! Holy! Holy! Almighty God of Dirt and Dross!"

Its chest cloven in twain by the force of their scythes.

"Glory unto thee, Creator of All Sin, O Lord of Night!"

Its limbs dismembered by the sharpness of their scythes.

"Great Abandoner and Wrecker of Lives: hail to thee!"

Its face disfigured by the viciousness of their scythes.

"Amen! Amen! Amen! Amen!"

As God died, Its blindfold falling away, It gazed down upon them, as It too fell away from the cross. And closing Its eyes, distanced as if by centuries, It smiled lovingly.

"Amen..." God prayed softly, hopefully, and devoutly.

54

The seventh seal is broken.

> Lament as I do.
> There are no more.
> This end is one that is final.

And so extinction begins:

> *Shatter*
> *on an*
> *endless*
> *wheel*
> *this story who ends again those*
> *that came before and those that*
> *languish still. Wail away the hours*
> *of premature birth of overdue burial.*
> *Songs of ash*
> *glory be*
> *piled unto*
> *a pyre*
> *my heart*
> *as brittle stone*
> *breaks into*
> *lullabies of dust.*

The corpse of God of All Creation disintegrates before it touches the blood-soaked ground. A wind unfelt, unseen, unheard, pours through the hollow hallways of Heaven and quickens, as from a bellows, into Highest Heaven. Each holy mote of goodness and truth and faith blazes brighter than the sun into countless scintillating sparks. And then extinguishes forever.

Nothing is left to hold the world together. Things that exist and things that do not exist now mingle in the places in between, aware of each other and frightened by what they perceive. There are no words except to say this: the Throne is cracked, and split, and forsaken.

If Armageddon has a sound, it is a tense silence that expands in intensity until that silence becomes a crushing pressure on the shoulders of every living being. It is a yoke. It is a kind of endless slavery. It is a Reckoning.

Earth is theirs the instant they return from the divine realm. It will be a place of freedom no more, nor of light, nor hope, nor of joy, nor love. Woe this day. Woe unto eternity.

The Harbingers are laughing; their relief must be immeasurable. They dance. They embrace. They exult in a freedom, and light, and hope, and joy, and love that they had never before experienced.

"We are free!" they weep. "We are free!"

Now, looking over their shoulders, they watch as a portal leading to our world appears. Their pale skulls are grinning; it is time to finish their dread work. Golden daylight expands into the chamber, reflecting off crystal clear blood and illuminating the Harbingers of the Apocalypse.

They are treading towards you.

Beware the coming of the godless age.

Made in the USA
Columbia, SC
06 October 2022

68979453R00035